HELL
IS
HUMANS

THE DIARY
OF SARTRE THE CAT

Does no one understand the plight of a cat in a human world ruled by an unfeeling Human God?

ISBN: 9798362807641

The more I see of humans,

the more I like cats... and even dogs.

ACKNOWLEDGEMENT

I would like to thank Dr. C. Buttigieg for her insightful contributions to the manuscript, detailed editing, and creative design.

Special thanks to Augie and Rubie for agreeing to participate in this project despite their distaste for felines. Their sacrifice does not go unnoticed.

THIS IS MY DIARY

Allow me to introduce myself... Who am I? Thoughtful of you to ask, even if it is simple human etiquette and who I am is of no great interest or concern to you.

My name is Sartre. Well, more to the absolute truth, that name has been bestowed upon me by my duplicitous captors. "Captors is a harsh term", you say. Not for them, even though it is unfathomable for them to recognize the civil boundaries of liberty they have crossed. They prefer the designation, "owners". I shall be writing much more about them throughout the course of my travail.

I remember little of how I came to exist in this human controlled world or any of the microcosmic details, including the jail in which I barely subsist. My distant past exists only as sparse memory of being ripped away from my tender mother at the helpless age of 12 weeks. I remember nothing of her except the warm, grey underbelly fur against which I nestled my head. Her anonymity is a shame from which I can never recover. The pain stretches the limits of my endurance. Excuse my lack of catposure when I relive the horror of this tragic event.

I was next thrust into a cold plastic and metal cage and transported to some unknown location where I was never to see my birth family again, at least to date. As for my father, I have yet to meet him or even discover his whereabouts. His existence is nothing more than an unidentifiable shadow figure. He is only referred to by these shameless humans as a philandering Tom. Nothing more descriptive has yet to be provided. As for my siblings, they likely suffered the same

1

fate as me. A miserable, bitter, undisclosed captivity no better than mine. I do not know any of them. It seems that I must come to accept that meaningful familial attachments will never transpire. Humans have robbed me and my family of them. Savages!

Do I still have your attention? Are you still interested, unremorseful human?

Of course, you are! Humans love to hear all about our feline adventures, even the petty details, since their own lives are consumed by nothing more than countless boring hours staring at screens of words and moving pictures. How lazy they are! I cannot ever imagine spending endless hours living through the narratives and eyes of others. I almost feel sorry for them. Almost, I say, if it wasn't for the anger boiling in my every breath over how I am barbarously treated.

Have no fear. You shall soon learn enough about me, and my friends. Well, not all, but many other felosophers who, like me, question the meaning of life.

The following pages contain a diary. No, not just any diary, but my own, "The Diary of Sartre the Cat". Have no doubt. You will read it. And I hope you weep for me as you vicariously experience the heartless life I am forced to lead. Although, I am unsure the human heart is capable of sympathy or empathy. Yes, this is my life summed up in words! Hopefully, you will not only read the pages but feel the desperation in my voice; the unforgiving attempt to untangle the meaning of my life and even existence itself.

Along the way I hope to meet at least a few intelligent like-minded felines. I hope they will share their stories too and I am sure you will be moved by their plight. Or perhaps not? After all, dear human, you interpret the world through your own self-motivated looking glass with little concern for us except to provide amusement, and in return you provide us the few necessities of life.

You may wonder why I decided to share with you my deep, personal experiences. You see, since I have little to no access to the lawful avenues of recourse created by humans for themselves and themselves alone, I have no choice but to document the horrors that I am being forced to face at the hands of my human oppressors. I believe that one day I will be vindicated and the only way to prove my allegations is to keep a detailed and thorough account of my experiences.

Therefore, I have decided to start a diary. This diary shall be the main source of evidence that will prove to everyone, one day, what the human world is doing to us, the cats of the world. It is, therefore, of paramount importance that you, the finder, forward this diary to the proper authorities for investigation. Do not think of destroying it: I have copies hidden in various places.

Hell isn't a place.
Hell is humans!

Photo source: Tima Miroshnichenko: https://www.pexels.com/photo/close-up-shot-of-atabby-cat-6234620/

BEGINNINGS

<u>Day 86:</u>   I have decided that indicating my days in confinement shall only help to bolster my claims of abuse. Here I am and it is Day 86. I believe I am now five or six months old, but my sprite age does little to console my despondency with the world thrust upon me. My captors seem to take great delight in punishing me with unbearable suffering. These monsters dine on the finest bone china while sitting on plush chairs beside lavishly decorated tables, ladened with such delicacies as steak, pork chops, ribs, and lamb. "What of my cuisine?", you smugly ask? I am forced to eat off a cold, dirty floor from a steel bowl filled with a can of stale, old grisly fish mixed with mushy cereal. This food comes out of a grimy can, and goes by misleading fancy names such as Kitty Delight, Yummy Tummy, Meowful Meals, etc. I assure you; the food is far from being a delightful feast. The ravenous canine in the house (who you will learn more about later) even tries to steal this rancid cuisine if I should turn my back. He clearly lacks the sophisticated palate and refined manners of a feline.

To make it worse, these jailors seem to get great pleasure out of coaxing me to eat this putrid mixture. They put it on their fingers and pretend it is yummy by making strange sounds like they themselves are eating and enjoying it. Once these monsters even resorted to rubbing some of this rank poison onto my lips in the hopes that I would accede to their demands. Fools! I hope the claw marks on the head jailors scrawny hands make her and the other jailors think otherwise.

I refuse to be broken! My greatest desire beyond survival is freedom. One day, I will succeed in making my escape. Till then, I must continue to document my time here and be satisfied with little victories of defiance. I hope my words can express the void I so acutely feel. In retaliation for their pathetic meals, I will make a note to eat their favorite houseplant tomorrow. Yes, it might make me sick. Ha! But I realize defiance and liberty have a price.

~ઈ.

Day 186:   Months and months of boredom speckled with days of torture. Escape for now still seems an impossible task. My best attempts to win their surrender seem futile. Ripping the leather couch, urinating on their slipcover, and knocking over a priceless porcelain vase has gained me nothing. Even my coup de grace, repulsing these oppressors by inducing myself to vomit on their imported Turkish rug, produced no tangible benefit. My line of attack must change. Yet, how?

I feel empty and cold, like stone!

Does no one understand the plight of a cat in a human world ruled by an unfeeling Human God, a God that doesn't care about us cats?

~ઈ.

Day 207:   I spent much of my time today sitting on the windowsill, enjoying the warmth of the sun's rays. There was nothing else to do. The humans went to work, and I was locked indoors. I had time to think as I watched groups of children walking home from school. A profound solution came to me. The answer to my plight has become so devilishly simple. I cannot imagine how it escaped me. Tomorrow night, I shall attempt to assassinate my captors by weaving a ball of blue yarn around their necks while they sleep in their beds at night. Ha, the fools think they have given me a toy and, so naively, they have provided me the means to their destruction. Freedom will prevail! Tomorrow, the cat known as Sartre shall taste victory and, with it, freedom.

~ఠ.

FAILED CATICIDE ATTEMPT

Day 209:   I write these sad words only a day after my brilliant idea of assassination came to a crashing failure. I spent most of yesterday sleeping under the sofa pillow, trying to save my energy to commit willful caticide. Unfortunately, my attempt using the ball of blue yarn proved to be a dismal failure. I could not create enough pressure to strangle my tormentors without them awakening and stealing it from me. It's a difficult task to achieve when one does not have fingers and thumbs. Realizing their foolish mistake, they swore at me, threw me out of the bedroom and locked the door.

Still, I cling to the relentless hope that my attempts are creating some torment for them. I have not given up hope! For the next week or so, I plan to sleep all day in my favorite claw marked leather chair and keep them awake all night with incessant meowing pleas for food. Perhaps, this will prove a significant thorn in their impudent bourgeois lifestyle. If not, I will certainly think up other means to exact my revenge. My mind is sharpened when liberty and freedom are the spoils of victory.

~🐾.

Day 225:   While surveying the basement for a portal of escape this evening, I had the fortunate luck (not for him) to come across a mouse scurrying across the concrete floor. Please do not be offended by the grotesqueness of my deed. Instead, appreciate his sacrifice. I came running up the stairs and brought my captors his lifeless, decapitated body in the hopes that I could ensure my release by showing them the ghastly deeds of which I am very capable.

Unfortunately, the mouse cadaver plan, like the others, backfired on me. I did nothing to convince them of the meaningless of existence without freedom. Rather than obtaining my predicted and well-earned release, they pitifully offered me condescending remarks such as "good boy," "keep up the good work," and "I knew he had the looks of a great mouser."

Imbeciles! At least the fools did provide me a few extra treats at bedtime tonight. Nothing as tasty as that mouse head they took away, though. It seems I have under-estimated my captors relentless desire to keep me confined. Not even exhibits of my feline savagery seem to be able to shake their resolve. I now clearly understand the solution to my freedom will lie in intelligence rather than brute ferocity.

~🐾.

I am Sartre the Cat
self-portrait
(date unknown)

Day 256:   My captor's ingenuity for torture seems to have no bounds. Do they not have any concept of how sadistic they are? Today, I was thrown into solitary confinement on the pretext that I was making some visiting human's allergies worse.

This pathetic human began sneezing all over the house as well as shedding water from his hollow eyes. His uncontrollable behavior had my captors scooping me up and putting me under lock down. Cowards! If this visitor could only have seen the murderous look in my eye, he no doubt would have made a hasty exit.

At this point in time, I do not know what allergies means, but whatever it is, it might prove useful in the future. *Note to self:* I must learn more about "allergies" and work them to my advantage.

~&.

AUGIE

Day 273:   My anger continues to grow like a tide drawn by a full moon. The other captives in the house seem insensitive to my plight. Augie, a pint size black and white canine with enormous ears so big you'd think he could use them like wings to fly. He is an obedience flunky whose only felosophy seems to be "I eat. Therefore I am." They say he is a rat terrier. Hmm, if his father or mother was a rat, I can easily understand the inherent acrimonious feelings I have towards him. As far as the terrier part goes, I gather it just means he likes to bolt around the house with reckless abandon. For what it's worth, he has mastered that quite well.

I realized early on, there is no use in confiding in such a beast and besides, he seems instinctively loyal to my captors. Also, his perverse habit of running around with a rubber chicken in his mouth is appalling and grates on my sense of civility.

In fact, this obsession with a mouth full of rubber chicken changes his whole demeanor. Suddenly, he morphs into a belligerent pit bull of a beast with the attitude of "come and take it, if you dare!" Cannot his captors at least provide a real meaty chicken, or even an undesirable leftover piece off their plates? No! Instead, they trick this humble canine into thinking he is the chicken king of the world and that a rubber one is something to be coveted. What type of human takes such advantage of an obviously mentally challenged animal, even if it is a pathetic canine? I do have a thought, though. Perhaps, if I pee on it, it could break this insane chicken mania?

Getting back to tactics, and more to the point, he will be of no use to me unless I can plan an escape that coincides with his daily release program called "walk". I have observed that our jailors regularly attach some bondage straps to his scrawny neck and force him to accompany them around the neighborhood, wagging his silly tail like some clown on a parade. This happens at least twice a day. Humans seem to have no boundaries of decency, and even I, Sartre the Cat, cannot help feeling somewhat badly for my simple-minded canine cellmate.

~ð.

BIRDS OF A FEATHER

DAY 312:   I woke up this morning and decided to explore another group of house captives who trouble me deeply: Lady Sunshine and Baby-Blue. They are two skinny, unappetizing budgies that I feel must be approached very cautiously. On first examination their treatment seems even more horrific than mine. I realize that is an almost unfathomable proposition to accept. Read on.

These two birds are housed in a small wire jail day and night. They are fed a diet of rotting seeds and water. The bottom of the jail has gritty stone to hurt their feet. There is a piece of stone on the side wall that allows them to scratch their beaks for entertainment. I cannot imagine living in such confined mind-numbing conditions except for one thing: Each day, they are allowed to taste partial freedom by being released from the cage and allowed to fly around their shuttered room. I must give them some credit for showing some honor and disdain for their treatment, by pooping on the humans' chairs and floor. For this, and only this, they do deserve some respect.

Still, there is something very unsettling about them. One of the two, Lady Sunshine, has mastered the human tongue.

Yes, I realize this stretches the bounds of my credibility, but you must listen. She converses with my captors daily. My first thought is that this miserable feathered bird is a mole - yes, a mole - undoubtedly planted by my captors to monitor

my whereabouts and report back on my every move. I suspect she is communicating to them my daily activities. Many times, I have witnessed Baby-Blue and Lady Sunshine grow immediately silent when I enter the room. Who knows what they gossip about, but I know it can't be good. They are not to be trusted. I must make a note to eliminate both of them. After all, you know what they say about birds of a feather. The metal barred jail cell that they are housed in will create a formidable challenge. Perhaps, I can enlist the help of Augie. "How?", you may ask. What if I can convince him these real birds are chickens? Wouldn't that be a very tasty treat, and far more of a delicacy than his ridiculous rubber chicken? It might prove to be a challenge since I do not speak Dog.

~🐾.

Day 368:   It has been over one year since my life in captivity began. An anniversary should be a time for great celebration, but mine is not. I have learned much over this time, but nothing significant enough to gain my release.

But, eureka! Finally, the answer finally came to me about a week ago. By refusing to use my litter box, a ridiculous plastic box full of clay grit, I have won partial periods of outdoor liberty.

Still, my captors hold much sway. The emptiness of my hunger forces me to return and accept their miserable offerings of food each evening. I am locked up at night with a contrived excuse that it is for my own protection from foxes and coyotes. The taste of partial freedom only motivates me more.

~🐾.

EVIL IN A WHITE JACKET

<u>**Day 392:**</u>   Is there no end to the malice my captors show me? Yesterday, I was thrown into a small plastic jail and driven to an unknown location. There, a strange evil woman dressed in white poked and prodded me, and forcefully stuck a needle into my backside. I overheard her say something about a rabies vaccine. I do not know what "rabies" is, but it seems just a pretext to allow my captors to inflict legalized torture. Perhaps she injected a microscopic disk to control me or even something to alter my DNA?

My slight consolation is the small piece of flesh from her arm that I still have stuck in my claws. The sight of her blood flowing invigorated me. Her foul deed did not go unpunished, and I rejoice in that. Even such small victories are cause for encouragement. I will never be assimilated by these pathetic humans. I returned home, exhausted. Despite my anger, I was just too tired to document this event right away.

I spent today resting on different parts of household furniture: the kitchen counter, the wooden bench in the front hall, and all cushions of their microfibre couch. I made sure I dropped bundles of fur on each area to annoy them. I still do not know who that woman in the white coat was, but they must have learned their lesson because I was left home alone most of today.

~ふ.

Day 408:   There is much cause for hope. On my daily freedom walks, I have finally encountered other felines of similar felosophical persuasion. Yes, cats with experiences and their own felosophy of life. They have interesting ideas just like mine. We share our experiences and insight. This intellectual stimulation gives me a new resilience. I am feeling stronger and bolder. When I admire myself in the mirror, I see a lion and not a human's "pussy cat". And, most importantly, I still refuse to abandon all hope as the human poet Dante wrote many years ago. Why? Because I have come to better understand the concept of Hell.

Hell isn't a place. Hell is humans!

~ふ.

EARLY FELOSOPHICAL ENCOUNTERS

Day 417:   What a groundbreaking day this has been! I observed another powerful feline walking the area called "the ravine" several times over the last few weeks. It is located about a mile from my jail and heavily populated with bush and trees. It has a foreboding look to it. I never have had the courage to approach and walk the trails. And yet, this feline I observe appears to be a leader. Not just a leader, but very magnetic in that he always has a group of fellow cats following him in procession. Sometimes, I even see them sitting around him in a circle, as if he is giving a lesson.

I am intrigued and fascinated by these meetings. I must be a part of the discussions. The next time I see them congregating, I will build up my resolve and courage to approach him and ask to join the group. In the meantime, I shall get a good night's sleep. I need to conserve my energy.

~ॐ.

Day 435:   What another momentous day! I do not even know where to begin. I had a fascinating discussion with a friend of mine, Zen, the next-door neighbor's chubby black and white long-haired feline and it certainly inspired me.

16

There is no denying his wisdom and so when the time came, I ventured down into the ravine where I saw a large cat with piercing green eyes walking and talking with what looked like his disciples. I crept up slowly with my body tense and low to the ground. I finally caught his attention. He stopped his dissertation in midsentence in order to carefully look me

over. The seconds seemed like hours, even for me who has little sense or use of human-made time constraints. My muscles were taut, and my hair was standing on end. I had the undecided appearance of fight or flight, yet I hoped for neither.

Finally the leader, whom I soon learned was named Machi[1], motioned for me to come forward, sit down, and join the group's discussion. I relaxed my muscles and calmly walked towards them and sat down in the circle. The other felines looked me over in a somewhat condescending way. I could sense they were

---

[1] Photo source: https://unsplash.com/photos/f4rYLkBy0gU

thinking: "Who is this newcomer, anyway?"

Machi made a hiss and cleared his throat to grab my attention. He asked me my name. I replied, Sartre. He seemed amused by this, shook his head, and I could see a smile break out at the corner of lips. I was not so amused when I saw the size of his canines.

"Welcome, Sartre", he said, and asked me to move and sit closer in front of him. The other cats looked me over once more with even greater scrutiny not knowing what to think of this young upstart. Did I deserve their acceptance?

Machi's expression suddenly changed when he noticed a piece of leather surrounding my neck with attached tags hanging down. He shook his head and viciously pointed his paw at me, while addressing the group. Then he shouted, "There you can see it all for yourself. Another feline wearing the bonds of subjugation." The others looked at me with scorn.

I cowered for a second and drew my body once again close to the ground. I was not sure what he was talking about, but it had something to do with the leather collar my humans insisted I wear. It had silver tags dangling down from it with my human's address and phone number etched into them. I often despised the thought of wearing such cheap jewelry when platinum or gold was more befitting of me. "What fools, these humans", I thought. As if I would ever forget where I lived and needed reminding. I think the other tag confirmed I had been tortured with needles. Ha, how ironic it is these mad humans worry about me losing myself when it is they who have lost their minds!

After a few seconds, I realized all the cats were intently staring at my neck as Machi kept pointing to it with his massive paw. It gave me a very unsettling feeling. I could hear whispers in the crowd suggesting I might be a spy for the humans. How insulting!

Machi finally lowered his paw and interceded. He said, "Please, everyone, remain calm." He looked into my cat eyes. "Luckily for you, my young, naive boy, you have come to the right place to learn about the garments you wear for your jailors."

I did not like him referring to me as "boy". It is true that I was only reaching maturity, but my mind was far ahead of my still growing body.

I remember the rest of the conversation with him vividly and will do my best to record as much of it here so I will never forget. I am sure I will refer to it many times in the future.

Machi explained to me that, "My captors gave me that name after trying out Bootsy, Stripe, Bugsy, Murphy, and Charlie. Fools! They came quickly to realize they were not dealing with such a mundane 'kitty' and so my name was changed early on to something more suitable. I believe it was shortened to Machi from Machiavelli. I live about one mile from here and host these get togethers weekly."

I made sure to smile at him trying to show I am in accord with his insubordinate attitude towards humans.

He continued looking at me as he explained the purpose of their meetings. I was delighted to find out that they often meet to discuss the plight of cats and ways our situation can be improved. He explained, "I have much experience, as do some of these other cats, and so we share ways to improve our existence and take advantage of these foolish humans."

I nodded in agreement. I decided to skip any more formalities. I was impatient like any young cat would be. I got to the crux of the matter. I prematurely blurted out, "How do you deal with our captors? Do you follow any felosophical principles?"

I remember him scratching his head with his front paw before answering: "Power is the key to a secure existence. One can never trust our captors so think like a cunning fox and act like a ferocious lion." He continued speaking while the others looked on with great concentration, even awe.

"You must live a double standard. One for you, and one for your jailors. Anything is right, as long as it is effective."

He pounded the ground with his paw and loudly spoke with greater force and conviction. "The end justifies the means."

I remember the group vigorously nodding at Machi and suddenly breaking out into chanting, "the end justifies the means, the end justifies the means, the end justifies the means..."

Machi allowed them a few moments to show this group unison, but then raised his paws to silence the group. Another cat asked him to give examples of that principle. Machi stood up showing off his shiny grey coat and athletic physique. He told us about his own experience.

"Number one. If you don't like the slop they feed you, don't just turn your nose up and walk off. Passive retreat will accomplish nothing. Cats are not Gandhi!"

Gandhi?

Gandhi? I had never heard this term before. I was perplexed and quickly interrupted: "What is a Gandhi?"

Machi looked at me and smirked. It turns out that Gandhi[2] is a skinny flea-bitten hairless cat who is a pacifist and despises any form of violence. Yes, he is a cat with many strange ideas. Some of the things he says make us appear weak and undetermined. For instance, Gandhi uses silly phrases, such as "the good feline is the friend of all living things."

---

[2] Photo source: наталья семенкова from Pexels:
https://www.pexels.com/photo/selective-focus-photography-of-sphinx-cat-lying-on-bedspread-991831/

"What nonsense!" shouted Machi. "Tell, that to the bird you are about to gobble or the mouse you just decapitated. As proof that Gandhi's felosophy is rubbish, the only think he has gotten in return for that pacifist ideology is his emaciated, beat-up body." Machi made sure the tone of his voice reflected contempt.

Machi returned to his original argument shaking his front paw back and forth.

"Listen well. I say you cannot be passive about your jailor's phony attempts to please your palate. If you are not satisfied, knock the bowl over and mess their floor! Jump on the table and try and steal something better! Repeat this until they have learned their lesson well and provide you better sustenance. Your treachery is not immoral, but necessary to make them change their minds about things. Cunning is paramount and nothing is off the table if it is effective. The end justifies the means!"

Oh, my goodness. The group, like a choir, immediately broke into the cadence, chanting once again, "The end justifies the means, the end justifies the means, the end justifies the means..."

Machi raised, then lowered, his paws to hush the group. "How do you think I have grown so magnificent in body and stature? Power and control are my weapons, dear friends. Why, they even treat me like a prince. And do you want to know a little secret, fellow cats?" I remember the group all leaning in with their ears perking up. Machi chuckled. "One of the little unschooled humans actually calls me 'The Prince'." There were a lot of meowing and cat calls at this point, cementing Machi's powerful influence, and he bowed in response with fake humility.

Machi then looked specifically at me, and I nodded that I understood what he was implying. It is true, I do understand his talk, but it all sounds so power-driven. Where is the morality of existence? And what about my freedom? I thought to myself, we all think we are free and in control, but aren't all of us just free in a human-created brick and mortar prison? That includes Machi.

At that point a belligerent looking member of the circle saw me in contemplation, rather than reverence, and gave me an annoying look. He stood straight up on his fours and raised a paw. I could see here was a tough outspoken black and brown tabby who was about to give us a fire branded speech. "You all know me." He then looked directly at me.

"Newcomer, my name is Nietzsche. Your question is well-purposed, if not naive, and I will try and help mold the conversation. Listen to me. There is no universal morality or freedoms. There are no facts, just interpretations. Cats are individuals and each must be judged as such."

He then began to shout that, "only the feelings of superior cats are important. That is the master morality." The group took up his words and began to chant. "Super cats, super cats, super cats…" He let this chorus shout out the chant for a short time and then motioned for them to stop. He went on for a few more minutes, but I distinctly remember his words because he spoke with such conviction and no remorse.

"It is impossible for a cat to suffer without making a human pay for it; every complaint already contains feline revenge."

The group then broke into a chant, "Make the humans pay. Make the humans pay. Make the humans pay…" and then they once again took up the chorus, "Super cats, super cats, super cats…"

Machi smiled and nodded at Nietzsche in agreement. Nietzsche returned the nod, then sat down, and allowed Machi to add further clarification.

"We do not need these humans. Surviving in the wild is innate in all of us. We simply choose to be housed and fed. We use them." A huge sardonic smile came over his face. "The irony of it all, is that they need us more than we need them."

Believe it or not, now the group broke into another chorus chanting, "They need us more. They need us more. They need us more..."

I was beginning to grow wearisome of all this cultish chanting of control and power. I mean, incessant meowed catch phrases are just cheap talk. Thankfully, before I could speak, another feline stood up. Krishna, popped up out of the back of the group. He asked for calm and stated that, "Truth was a pathless land." He looked proud of himself until Machi motioned for him to sit down, close his jaws, and keep his felosophical "pathless" rants to himself.

Machi quickly added an abridgement to Krishna's narrative: "Truth is not pathless. Truth is what we cats interpret it to be – not humans."

I wonder why a cat like Krishna[3] had even bothered to join

[3] Photo source: Tamba Budiarsana from Pexels:
https://www.pexels.com/photo/stretching-white-cat-979247/

this group's discussion, but I can see that he is a compassionate fellow trying to bring reason to such a dogma shouting rabble.

After a few more hours of discussing power, control, and Super Cats, The Prince (I mean, Machi) dissolved the meeting and we all headed home for our dinners. I remembered to poop along the way so I would not have to dirty my paws in that foul smelling gritty litter box my humans so ungraciously provide me. Perhaps, I will pee on their rug first thing in the morning since all those speeches I heard today make me feel powerful and rebellious.   But now, I must stop writing. This long entry feels like it is giving me catpal tunnel.

~ಠ.

Day 437:   So, it is the weekend and while my captors get a break, I do not. I remain a subject of their cruel desires to objectify me. They treat me like a toy for their amusement. Today was no exception. They spent most of the afternoon taunting and tormenting me with grotesque little pieces of fur they drag around the floor, hoping to attract my attention. Their efforts are deplorable. I refuse to participate in such foolish games. I will never capitulate and their annoyance at my complete disregard provides me great satisfaction.

The loyal canine, Augie, just views these childish toys as another possible food source. Perhaps he will puke it up in their bathroom later tonight or tomorrow morning. If not, I plan to throw up a hairball in their bathtub just in time for their abhorrent water ritual. Should they ever try the water ritual with me, I will swear out an oath of murderous vengeance.

~𝔇.

Day 478: I must say the felosophy of Machi and his group continues to grip my imagination. I decided not to write for a while so I can reflect on all that I heard. In the meantime, I have been spending time looking at my bondage collar in the mirror and the humiliation runs inside me like a waterfall. Yet, Machi's felosophy still weighs heavily on my sense of morality. Power, deception, and treachery seem like useful tools to control my jailors. But something is missing. Why is there no joy or the happiness of life being discussed?

Fortunately, I was able to discover such a felosophy yesterday, while walking in the backyard of a house a few hundred yards away. It is a sacred and hallowed tree lined yard with a surrounding wooden fence. You ask, "Why is this space special?" This backyard has always been a killing ground for me and others. It houses a small wood building on a stake filled with seeds and nuts. Nothing that would excite my palate or any other sane felines, for sure, but it attracts all kinds of birds.

It is marvelous! I can sit under a nearby bush for hours, watching all different types of birds fighting for positions on the stand to access the food. The mourning doves are especially enticing since they come to ground to feed. Imagine, coming to ground? Silly and docile birds that are easy to surprise and, I might add, quite tasty.

My friend, a bloated brown and white tabby named Epicurus[4], lives here and he has tried to make me believe that the prime good in life was pleasure and avoiding suffering. He often sits motionless in a nearby shrub, waiting for his next victim, usually one of those moronic doves.

Epicurus is well-fed but takes pleasure in the hunt. Matching wits with a few hungry pee-brained birds does not seem like much of a challenge to me, but Epicurus can sit under that bush for hours, soaking in the thrill of the kill. He reminds me of those insane humans who sit for hours by a river hoping a fish will miraculously attach to their long sticks.

The felosophy of Epicurus, I must say, seems superficially attractive. For at many times in my short life I have feasted on doves, sparrows, and even a jay, not out of necessity, but for the pleasure of the hunt. That felosophy at first seemed appealing, until yesterday when I met one of his

---

[4] Photo source: https://unsplash.com/photos/WOfj1fmkxbg

acquaintances, named Zeno[5].

Zeno is a large well-muscled Maine coon who seems to face all his trials with courage and dignity. For him, the highest good is a life of virtue, temperance, and courage. Quite a stoical felosophy!

Not to say he wouldn't kill, but here is the difference. Killing is out of hunger and need, and not pleasure. He has no need to show off his hunting skills or acrobatics, though he has perfected them. He accepts his humans without the same prejudices most of us do. His life of stoicism means accepting any fate that is bestowed upon him. Bad food is accepted without complaint. Scratching his humans and inflicting pain on them is done without remorse. There is much to be said for such an uncomplicated ethical life. He

---

[5] Photo source: Lera Mk from Pexels: https://www.pexels.com/photo/furry-cat-sitting-on-the-ground-10480346/

seems the opposite of Epicurus, whose fault can be gluttony. But Zeno is at risk of slipping into hypocrisy and doing unintentional things he says are wrong of others.

Epicurus and Zeno are at two ends of the spectrum, but still do not fulfill my felosophical needs. A part of my being remains empty, and I need to continue my search for life's meanings. My human captors better not get in my way. It was a fascinating discussion. The only problem was that all our meowing scared the birds away and I was not able to enjoy such a delicacy.

~ఈ.

A FRIGHTFUL EXPERIENCE

Day 533: I must say I have been in the doldrums for several weeks now. I frequently think about the words of Machi and Nietzsche and have even tried out some of their methods on my humans. But achieving a few short-term goals of better food, drink and bedding does not seem to answer my burning questions about the meaning of my feline life.

Why am I here? To eat, pee, poop, and survive in this meaningless world just to be tormented by my humans? Surely there is more to existence than just this. I will not give up my quest for meaning.

Meanwhile, the humans celebrated something called "Halloween" the other day. I remember them having the same celebration around this time last year. I was excited at first, thinking it was a celebration for me as they decorated the house with beautiful silhouettes of cats in black and orange. I thought they may have turned over a new leaf and finally recognized the honor of having me in their presence. But then, I realized that it was just some ritual my humans were performing that included a bunch of strangers coming to our door demanding treats. This torment of hearing the doorbell ring from time to time is nothing compared to what I endured that evening.

I was forced to wear clothes and not just any regular shirt and tie. They put me in a costume. I looked like a pumpkin. I don't even like pumpkins. Foolish Augie had foam pieces attached to the side of his body to look like something they call a "hot dog". There was nothing hot about it. He looked like a bad snack, which was quite suitable for him. They laughed and took photos of me. Whoever is reading this: There is photographic proof out there. It was one of the most humiliating experiences of my life. I must remember the date so I can stay hidden in the ravine for that 24-hour period next year... unless I manage to find permanent freedom by then. *paws crossed*

~🐾.

DAY 546:   The weather has been atrocious the last week. We are coming close to what humans call deep winter. I know by the awful cold white stuff that coats my walking trails. It sticks to my paws and makes me ache. There are some advantages though. I can splash up my captor's floors with dirty water. I have even seen one slip on the puddles of liquid I have left behind and that gives me pleasure. Augie, like all dumbfounded canines, just laps it up like it is an aged fine wine. How uncivilized!

Another thing I always notice this time of the year is that there are less birds around and those that remain here become keen, almost desperate, to attend the seed houses perched atop their poles. Their hunger makes them less attuned to sense our whereabouts. Yes, there is good hunting when the white stuff falls, so all is not lost. My gluttonous friend, Epicurus, rejoices when he sees the white stuff fall. He knows his hunting season will be very fruitful.

Mind you, the white stuff does create a real problem for my education. My captors make it more difficult for me to stay out or trek any distance. If I am gone more than a few hours, they come out looking for me, calling my name.

"Here Sartre. Come Sartre. Where are you, boy?"

What fools!

Do they think their feeble attempts to rob me of my daily freedom will work? I stayed out all night one day last week only to find ridiculous mug shots of me plastered all over the neighborhood light poles and mailboxes the next morning. I was mortified! The photo used was a terrible likeness. I am far more handsome than how I am depicted in the photo these devils used. When I did return, my captors punished me by taking away my outdoor privileges for a few days. Beasts! Not to worry. They were rightfully punished by me puking on their favorite comforter. I heard them swearing, saying it had to be taken to a special cleaner. I am proud of my resistance.

MORE FELOSOPHICAL ENCOUNTERS

DAY 555:   It has been weeks since I have been able to turn my thoughts back to learning about life and its mysteries. I think I am suffering from pumpkin PTSD. The very sight of a pumpkin is nauseating and makes my hair stand on end. Now, I aim to torment my humans with atrocious manners daily, but I seem to derive less pleasure from it. There is something about Machi and Nietzsche's felosophies that do not resonate well with me. Perhaps they did before, but not now as I mature. I sense I am becoming calmer and more of an intellectual as I age. I have avoided the ravine, so that I do not cross paths with Machi or Nietzsche, at least for the time being.

I went out for a stroll today. It was quite chilly. The humans in the neighborhood have started decorating their personal abodes with colorful twinkly lights. I do not understand the purpose of this. I ran into my friend, Zen, just as I approached the corner. He recognized my gloomy psyche. He rescued me with wise advice he had heard spoken by an old cat-sage that had come from a faraway land which, according to rumor, is a place called "Tibet". "There are only two mistakes one can make along the road to truth: not going all the way, and not starting."

I believe Zen is right. I must not give up. I must continue to pursue my truth in life even if I do not know where I am going or what I will find. To that end, Zen said he will organize a meeting with a few other felosophers he knows and of whom he has spoken so thoughtfully.

In a few days, I will meet with Descartes, Kant, and

Schopenhauer (nicknamed "Shopsy" by his humans) in the park down the street. I hope I can learn more from these wise cats than just gluttony, treachery, deception, power, and violence.

~ᛘ.

DAY 561:   This is the day I thought might change my life forever; the day I met Descartes, Kant and Shopsy. Although Zen has praised them, I got the impression he feels they are too dogmatic for his taste. I need to decide that for myself.

I walked into the park noting a few young humans playing on a swing set. They were seated and going back and forth for no apparent purpose. Typical of human behavior; most of what they do has no purpose. They certainly were not going anywhere which seemed to me like a lot of effort for nothing in return. They reminded me of a hamster running nowhere on that silly wheel. They saw me but took no notice of me. There were three cats talking to each other about 50 yards off to the side. They noticed me coming up the walkway and each gave me a careful look over. One, a large ginger tabby, motioned for me to come sit down with them.

His name is Descartes. He spoke to me and, as is my custom, I am writing down his exact words in this diary after our meeting.

He bowed and whispered, so I had to listen carefully, "COGITO, ERGO SUM CATTUS."

I looked puzzled at him. I speak Catish and understand some

English, but this language was unfamiliar to me. What was he saying? "It is Latin," he said, sensing my lack of understanding. He rephrased his sentence in Catish, so I could understand: "I think, therefore I am cat!"

Descartes[6] paused, allowing his words to sink in, before continuing. "Zen has spoken fondly of you, and we agreed a meeting might prove fruitful. We understand you are on a quest for the meaning of a cat's life. I applaud your veracity. Most felines seem to be content to follow the gluttonous rantings of Epicurus, or the volatile expressions of Machi and Nietzsche."

I asked if he knew these felosophers. "Of course, we know them. And we do not dismiss any view of life until it is fully analyzed and tested. Machi makes several interesting points, and I cannot say he is neither wrong nor right. For instance, he believes humans are unnecessary and are to be

---

[6] Photo source: https://unsplash.com/photos/6SqLTK98OS4

used for gain. In some respects, his distrust is well-appreciated. My own view on that matter is to be more selective." He summed up his view as follows:

- "To know what humans really think, pay regard to what they do, rather than what they say."

- "The senses deceive from time to time, and it is prudent never to trust wholly those humans who have deceived us even once."

I countered how difficult it was to decide which differing felosophy was right.

He quickly answered, "If you choose not to decide, you still have made a choice. Because reason is the only thing that makes us cats and distinguishes us from the other beasts and mindless humans. I believe reason exists, in its entirety, in each of us cats." Descartes then looked over at Kant, as if to pass off the torch.

Kant then looked at me and asked if he could speak directly. I nodded but quickly my curiosity got the better of me and I broke in: "How did you get the name Kant?"

He burst out laughing. "It is a funny story and not what you think. These moronic humans. They tell me 'Kant you stay off the couch! Kant you stop playing with the rug! Kant you stop unraveling the toilet paper!... Kant... Kant you... Kant you...' So, I decided my name must be Kant! The captors call me some other laughable names to torment me, like Silky, which I completely ignore. Well, not completely. I sometime allow the young unschooled humans to get away with Silky, if I am in a kind, compassionate mood."

Kant[7] went on, "I understand how impressive the large following a cat like Machi or Nietzsche commands, but it is not relevant. Seek not the favor of the multitude of cats; it is

seldom got by honest and moral means. But seek the testimony of few wise cats (he said that while looking over at Descartes and Shopsy) and number not their voices but weigh them."

Shopsy then jumped up on a bench, and looking down, interrupted Kant to weigh in.

"Dear Sartre, my new friend. Do not be afraid to face the difficulties of life without having a multitude of followers. To live alone is the fate of all great cats."

---

[7] Photo source: İdil Çelikler from Pexels: https://www.pexels.com/photo/brown-tabby-cat-on-gray-concrete-floor-13697617/

I broke in and asked, "But what of the humans? What do you think and feel on the subject?" He smiled and easily said, "I believe all a cat's sorrows spring out of their relations with humans. And, why? Because it is humans who inflict on a cat their worst enemies: pain and boredom."

Shopsy[8] then proceeded to put his paw on my shoulder before complimenting me: "The more unintelligent a cat is, the less mysterious existence seems to them. You have done well to reach this level of questioning, young feline."

Suddenly, the cats came to attention and looked out across the playground. Meandering towards them was a long striding Calico.

"Oh, Oh!" said Shopsy. "Here comes Kierkegard. We call him Kierky."

[8] Photo source: Bayram Yalçın from Pexels: https://www.pexels.com/photo/cat-sitting-on-grass-13279313/

"Kierky?" I asked in puzzlement.

"Yes," said Kant. "He's got some strange ideas, but we'll let him tell you about them."

Kierky[9] walked up to the group and greeted each cat individually like they were his brothers. He finally looked over at me and asked, "Shopsy, do we have a new student in this youngster?"

Descartes and Kant nodded, while Shopsy said, "Go easy on him, Kierky. He's had to take in a lot of new information already."

"Ha, ha. Yes, it is a difficult subject. Truth is subjectivity, not axioms or systems." Kierky called out.

Before he could continue, I said that his words resembled something I heard a cat named Krishna talk about.

"Yes, yes. You mean truth is a pathless land. He's somewhat

---

famous or infamous with that line. But, in some respects I would have to agree. But do you know what the real secret is, Sartre?"

I shook my head, while the other scholarly cats looked at each other knowing what felosophical punch line was to come.

"A cat's life can only be understood backwards, but it must be lived forward."

But how does that obvious timeline help anything, I wondered to myself. Descartes could see I was growing weary and broke in and relieved the strain. He said we probably have had enough discussion for the day. He suggested I return home while the others would continue some more discussion.

I thanked and promised to keep in touch, but I was finding this all very confusing. I still do. I really do not see much difference in the views espoused by Machi and Nietzsche versus Descartes, Kant and Shopsy. Yes, the level of analysis, violence and deception differs, but all make it clear the humans are a dangerous, inferior species. I cannot disagree with that. Perhaps there is more toleration in one camp, but not what I hoped will be my ultimate answer.

Perhaps there is another approach to take. One day I must find the time to seek a melting pot of felosophy and feligion. Perhaps, the answers will have to be partially found in faith and hope rather than analysis, rules and experience. Once again, I hope Zen could guide me on this path. He probably has others with whom I can engage in deep talks.

I am exhausted. I spent most of evening running away from my humans. They chased me all around the house until they finally managed to corner me next to the bookshelf in the study. While I was frightened at first, there was a moment of hope when I realized they were removing the leather piece Machi called a bond of subjugation. The moment of hope was fleeting as they immediately replaced the leather with a red velvet and white faux-fur band. I had an automatic flashback of the same thing happening this time last year. I realized it was a season the humans call "Christmas", and everything had to be decorated, including me.

Their cruelty knows no bounds. Even Augie was embarrassed. He was forced to wear a red bow that the humans called "festive". That is the same thing they said about my bow last year. I felt a little pity for that dog.

The one good thing about Christmas is that they gave me a gift last year, if you can call it that. How generous! I was given a battery-operated fake fur mouse on wheels that I was supposed to chase. Why do they torment me with such childish toys? Can I expect anything better this year? Ha, my gift to them will be to tear up their favorite antique doll.

That is it for tonight. I am exhausted. My catpal tunnel is acting up.

~&.

FESTIVE FURY

DAY 583:   It has been an exasperating and hectic week. If my calculations are correct (and they always are), their festive season should be over in a few days. In the meantime, my humans have been continuing with their rituals of abominably decorating the house and singing about some unusual creatures called "reindeer" with ridiculous names like Rudolph, Blitzen, Comet and Vixen. They must be members of some cult who come out at this time of year. It is quite scary, to be honest. The names Blitzen and Vixen makes my hair stand on end. I have seen pictures of these weird looking reindeer. Why do they have trees growing out of their heads? Would Augie try and mark their heads? I'd like to see that! I still haven't been able to figure out the reason for all this colored green and red stuff. Maybe red represents the blood that they suck from my life? Who knows!

They put a tree - can you imagine a real tree - in the living room? I am so confused by this. If they want to be with a tree, why don't they just live outside? I think Augie is also confused as I saw him lift a leg at the trunk base to mark his territory. I smiled in satisfaction knowing how upset the humans were going to be when they realized what he had done. That canine can be quite helpful at times when he is not thinking about how to please the captors.

Earlier this evening, I observed the two adult humans wrapping a bunch of items in colorful paper. I tried my best to see what they were hiding, but I had to keep my distance for my own safety. When I get too close, they try to get me to sit on their lap. It is another way for them to control me. I hate them stroking my head like I am some kitten in need of coddling. Some of the items they were wrapping were as big as the metal and plastic cage they put me in when they want to take me somewhere. That worried me. Other items were so small. I figured they might be listening devices or implants they would use in the future to monitor me. I realized I had to be brave and investigate further after everyone went to sleep. It was of utmost importance to the feline world.

As soon as I started to hear the male human snoring like the beast he is, I knew the coast in the living room was clear. I tip-toed down the hall and made my way to where all those wrapped packages were placed ever so strategically under that pine tree near the front window. I first encountered the odor of Augie's pee which made me gag and threw my scent off a bit. Once I recovered, I carefully sniffed each package, looking for clues that may indicate its contents. I got nothing. I placed my ear against them, listening for any sounds indicating that something alive or mechanical was inside. Again, I got nothing. I had no choice but to use the claws I was given. I tore apart all that colorful paper and, to my confusion, discovered a number of mundane items, including pyjamas, a tea kettle, and a toy car. Thank Cat God there were no fake mouses or furballs they expect me to drag around. The only thing I discovered to my pleasure was some biscuits and milk left on the coffee table. I devoured them, of course. I prefer shortbread, but the oatmeal will do. It is time for me to go to my hiding place. I overheard the adult humans telling the young ones about some old unshaven bum named Santa coming over tonight by sneaking in through the chimney. What the fluff? Apparently, he sees everything. It definitely sounds sketchy, so I think it is wise to keep my distance. Maybe, Augie can make himself useful for once and pee on the intruder if he appears dangerous.

~𝔡.

DAY 591: I write this in the very early hours of the morning, not to my delight. I must document this event as further proof of the suffering I must endure of the hands of my human oppressors. While I was sound asleep, I was awakened by the obnoxious screeches of my humans: "Happy New Year! Happy New Year!"

What the fluff does that mean? And who cares? What is a year but just another useless human time construct? And, what if it is new? Why do they have to announce it to everyone? Surely their fellow humans know what day it is. I am not happy! So, catpoop to "Happy New Year".

Now I am awake and since I cannot fall back asleep due to my intense fear of being so abruptly awakened once again, I have decided to express myself in writing so that future generations of feline will be better prepared than me to deal with this specie of savage animal.

~𝔡.

I MEET AN INSPIRING QUEEN

DAY 598:   Well, this year might be a happy one after all. This was the chance meeting that would change my life forever. I met with a beautiful intelligent Queen (For those unschooled humans who may be reading this, a Queen is a term for a mature female cat). Her intellect is the equal of mine and her ideas are far ahead of her time. I was out for my morning walk. It was cold but I am fortunate to be blessed with luscious thick hair that keeps me warm. As I was strutting my stuff down the catwalk, I saw a beautiful white, long-haired feline just ahead of me. She strode with confidence and did not notice me as she was deep in thought. I approached, waved my paw at her, and asked her name. She stopped, looked me over, decided I was no threat to her, and then said it was Simone.

I began some typical feline small talk, like asking how she liked her kibble, whether she has seen any good birds lately, whether she knows some good hunting trails, etc. I must say I am not good at mundane chit-cat and much prefer deeper intellectual discussion, so this was quite the challenge. She tolerated my feeble banal diatribe for a few minutes, but it did not seem to be of any interest to her. I could see I was not making a good impression. She looked bored. Rightly so because I was boring myself.

I took a chance and tried a different approach. I blurted out, "Have you ever met Machi and what do you think of him?"

That immediately caught her attention. Her whole expression changed. Her eyes became inflamed, her ears pricked up, and she gave a low-pitched growl. "You mean that misogynist, neanderthal cat?" she bluntly responded. I liked her feistiness.

I nodded in agreement, or more to the point, not to incense her anger any worse. There was an obvious dislike which she purposely did not try to hide.

She continued, "That bully describes males as dominating, and us females as weak. He has the typical sexist intolerances of our gender. We are mere objects for which the male controls and protect. He thinks we are incapable of becoming leaders and likens females to property and ownership."

I had to applaud her. She is a Queen in every sense of the word. I too feel Machi's ideal state is not my own, but I never realized how left out females were until she pointed it out. I liked her fire, and I was intrigued at what I was hearing. I decided to press her further on other felosophers I had encountered. "Have you heard of Descartes?"

She rolled her eyes and looked at me like I was a dim cat. "Who hasn't?"

I felt sheepish, but asked her, "So what do..." She didn't let me finish.

"Descartes is a genius. His argument that females have equal capacity to reason, because reason operates independently of the body is brilliant. Also, he believes in gender equality which is grounded in the doctrine of the equality of feline souls. Isn't it obvious to all, without all the sexist tom foolish rantings of Machi and Nietzsche?"

She added confidently, "In a pride of lions, who does the hunting? Who cares for the young? Of course, lionesses are the equal of any of those lazy males. Do you think a pretty mane denotes anything more than an overdeveloped narcissism?"

I had really got her going on a topic that was clearly dear to her heart. "Please, Simone. Slow down." I implored her. "I'm not the bad cat here. I also think Machi and Nietzsche aren't anyone's answer." I was glad she looked appreciative and continued her enlightening discussion.

Simone went on to identify herself as an existentialist cat. She stated that it is the only felosophy that takes on challenging the false premise that without a Cat God, everything is permissible. It is true, cats are alone in the world and that we exist without guarantees. However, there is also the existence of our freedom that contests the terrors of a world ruled only by the authority of human power.

She went on to say we begin our lives as kittens who are dependent on others and embedded in a world already endowed with a cat's purpose. It is a ready-made human world of values and established authorities. This is a world where obedience is demanded of kittens and cats. As kittens, we are, in effect, learning the lessons of freedom, that we are our own creators of the meaning and value of the world. Kittens experience the joys, but not the anxieties of freedom. Simone said that kittens believe that the foundations of the world are secure and that their place in the world is naturally given and unchangeable. Adolescence marks the end of this idyllic era. Emerging into the world of adults, cats are now called upon to renounce the human world, to reject the mystification of kittenhood and to take responsibility for our choices. Some of us evade the responsibilities of freedom by choosing to remain kittens; that is, to totally submit to the authority of humans.

Simone acknowledged that, "human authority is necessary for the kitten's survival. However, to treat adults as kittens is immoral and evil. And, if we are exploited, enslaved and terrorized, how can our lack of submission to authority of the humans be counted as an act of bad faith? Freedom is not hiding behind the authority of humans or establishing ourselves as authorities over others. That is offensive."

I hope this would be just one of a multitude of meetings with this brilliant Queen.

~🐾.

DAY 615: I am writing this first thing in the morning, even before I consume the stuff humans call cat food. I had a wonderful dream. It was about Simone. I dreamt that she would one day consider me more than just a friend. Who knows? There are no guarantees of a cat even having a next breath in this corrupt human world, but I shall hold onto this deep desire with optimism. Catentine's Day is approaching on the 14th next month. Maybe I will make my move with Simone on the most catmantic day of the year.

I'm signing off now. Nature calls.

~ঠ.

DAY 679: It has been a while. I have met up with Simone a few more times since our initial meeting. Our rendezvous are not as frequent as I hope as my humans have held me hostage even more nowadays because of the exceptionally cold weather this winter. Simone seems to make my days more tolerable despite my human interactions being a source of great misery.

~ঠ.

I MEET SADE AND MARX

DAY 698: The weather is warming up and the cold white fluff that covers the ground is disappearing. I was able to get out for some fresh air. Humans smell so bad. I often gag when they try to kiss me.

I met with two cats, and while they send shivers up my spine like Simone, it is for a very different reason. I will tell you their names more as a warning than introduction: Sade and Marx. Yes, be careful when you approach these cats for their ideology can be dangerous despite the best of intentions.

How do I begin? Meeting with these two polar opposites was purely by chance and not one I would like to repeat. Some cats say there is no chance and nothing is coincidence. Perhaps?

I had heard of Sade when I walked the parking lots near my human's prison. There was much talk of this libertine Tom, who walked the deserted streets at night and took liberties with many of the females in the neighborhood. No one new how many kittens this player cat had fostered. He must stay away from Simone if he knows what's good for him. Nonetheless, there was something enticing to me about the absolute freedom ideology this cat exhibited. No one had ever seen him with a human. I believe the captors use the term feral - a cat completely independent and free of human bondage. At first thought, it sounded almost miraculous.

I decided earlier today that I would stay out late, track him down, and approach him. I found him in a restaurant parking lot where he had been looking for scraps. Perhaps, a few leftovers had fallen out of the bins onto the concrete and provided a nice evening snack for him.

I came out of the shadows and stood under a light pole at the side of the lot. He quickly turned towards me, looked me over quite aggressively, but quickly realized I was no threat. He motioned for me to approach, but made it clear he was not sharing any of his tidbits. I told him I was not interested in food but speaking with cats about their felosophical approach to life. I was especially interested in his ideas that I had heard so much about. I thought flattery might be the way into this cat's psyche.

He smiled, stopped his munching, sharpened his claws on the concrete and after a brief pause decided it would be interesting to engage in my education. Maybe he could teach me something, he must have thought. I was dubious given the beast-like life he led, but still interested in what he had to say.

"I am Sade[10]," he said in boastful fashion. "You no doubt have heard of me," he continued stroking his whiskers with pride. "I am an existentialist cat, but most of all, I believe in absolute freedom. Some dislike me because I have uncovered and preached the erotic feline secrets. Others

[10] Photo source: https://unsplash.com/photos/TQ0XD_mGC8c

have said I have an unavailable utopian appeal to freedom."

His bravado started to irritate me. I felt compelled to break in. "I too believe in freedom. You are not alone with the concept. But I believe you have perverted the meaning of freedom. You act like a great moralist but are endorsing unsatisfactory ethics with your constant carousing at night, impregnating any female cat you meet, and then abandoning them. Shall I go on?"

Sade hissed at me. "I have heard the things you speak of about me, but human cruelty reveals to each cat the particularities and ambiguities of our conscious and fleshed existence. There are always tyrants and victims, even with cats. My account of human cruelty provides a convincing critique of their social, political and personal hypocrisies. But theirs is a perversion of freedom and an exploitation of our vulnerabilities."

I countered that it is clear we assume responsibility for one's choices, as a necessity, but it is not sufficient to just satisfy the existential ethics of freedom. In the end, I told Sade he mistook power for freedom, and misunderstood the meanings of being a whole ethical cat.

"Sade, you substitute the spectacle of a Roman coliseum for the real-life experiences and accept fake transactions of domination and assimilation for genuine relationships. This lacks true equality and generosity."

I must say, I have surprised myself. I now am offering up my own existential felosophy rather than just being quiet and acting like a recording machine.

Sade was unimpressed with my remarks, and disrespectfully marked the pole I was standing by with his pee. I think he wanted to swat me too, but perhaps my hiss made him think twice. I thought, "What a lascivious lout. I should fight him!" But since I do not like violence, at least against a fellow feline, I decided to just step back and carefully watch him slink away into the shadows.

I noticed that Sade soon spotted a beautiful calico feline at the other end of the parking lot and trotted off looking for his next mistress. Hopefully, not more unwanted kittens. Good riddance of him.

~ঌ.

DAY 712:   It has been about two weeks since meeting Sade and, unfortunately, I haven't been out since. My human jailors considered two-weeks' confinement a just punishment.

What a travesty of justice! There is never any right of appeal for an imprisoned cat. However, they shall not stifle my longing for freedom no matter what locked doors and bonds they place upon this magnificent body.

~ঌ.

TIME SERVED

DAY 713:   At last, out on my first day of freedom, I had the opportunity to meet a cat I had heard all about throughout the neighborhood, Marx[11]. He is considered more of a revolutionary than a felosopher, and a bit of a "whack cat" at that. I do not let that bother me. Aren't most rebel and revolutionary cats considered a bit "off" in the beginning?

He was standing outside a fish store smelling the sidewalk, perhaps looking for a few scraps of catfish. I walked up and introduced myself. He responded by welcoming me. "Good afternoon, comrade."

"What's a comrade?" I thought to myself?

It didn't take very long for him to tell me about his ideas. It is his contention that working cats of the world need to unite. We are all just being valued by our humans as a utility and thrown aside by the very evil ones once our days of worth are used up.

"We need to cut the chains of our bondage from these bourgeoisie captors!" he shouted, hoping other cats looking

---

[11] Photo source: Pixabay from Pexels: https://www.pexels.com/photo/low-angle-shot-of-a-tabby-cat-208984/

on nearby might take up his cause. Instead, they shook their heads and moved away.

Marx went on to explain how he is increasingly becoming preoccupied with understanding the human's capitalist mode of production, as driven by a remorseless pursuit of profit and whose origins are found in the extraction of surplus value from the exploited proletaricat.

He went on to tell me about a kind of fairness in that he believes each cat should live according to his abilities and be blessed with what is according to his needs. He called this cat-munism.

"I think that catitalism is unjust. Catitalist profit is ultimately derived from the exploitation of the worker cat. Catitalism's dirty secret is that it is not a realm of harmony and mutual benefit, but a system in which one class of cat systematically extracts profit from another at the urging of humans. How could this fail to be unjust?" he said.

Marx also shared his own view of God. I shall not forget these words. "A Cat God is the meow of the oppressed creature, the heart of a heartless world, and the soul of soulless conditions. It is the cat nip of the average cat."

Quite a meowful if I do say so myself. But what did he mean?

Marx said that cats invented God in their own image. He argues that worshipping a God diverts felines from enjoying their own cat powers. In their imagination, cats raise their own powers to an infinite level and project them onto an abstract entity. Hence, feligion is a form of alienation. It separates cats from "our highest species' evolutionary essence."

As I initially stated, this cat was pretty much out there. I don't buy much of what he is selling, but I do want to dig deeper, so I showed interest by asking, "But why do cats fall into feligious alienation?"

Marx smiled and felt invigorated by having an interested audience even if it only numbered one cat. He explained that feligion is a response to alienation in material life and, therefore, cannot be removed until a cat's material life is emancipated from his human captors. At that point, feligion will wither away.

For me, it kind of sounds like who needs a divine savior after one is saved from the intolerable humans?

I finally had to leave before dark and head back to my cell or else my jailors would impose another round of forced confinement. I wished him well, sensing I was not in-tune with his felosophy and would likely not see him again.

He responded with: "Good luck, comrade, on your quest. Power to the felines! Down with the human bourgeoisie."

It gives me a lot to think about.

In the meantime, I smell something deliciously fishy coming from the kitchen and I must investigate.

~&.

I MEET A DIVA DOG *eye-roll*

DAY 724: As a further example of their narcissism, humans insist on celebrating themselves whenever they can. Today was no exception. Humans like to make themselves the center of attention, including when it comes to things over which they have no control, like their birth. I knew there was trouble when I woke up this morning and noticed colorful balloons, streamers and birthday greetings all over the living room. I had to get away, but the humans refused to let me outside. I jumped on top of the kitchen cabinets, using the countertop as leverage. I had an excellent view from there so I can see anyone approaching before they could see me.

As soon as I heard the doorbell ring for the third time within five minutes, I knew it could only mean one thing: the humans were gathering in great numbers to hold some sort of birthday ritual that includes singing out of tune and eating something called "cake". It must be something delicious because they would never let me have a taste as they lick their forks clean. At the same time, they try to set the cake on fire! *sigh* Humans make no sense.

Just when I thought things could not get worse, the utmost unpleasant odor filled the room, hitting my nose like a brick. It could only mean one thing: Another canine had entered the premises. I was officially outnumbered. There were at least two dogs on the property now, including Augie. No sooner did I get a whiff of that revolting canine odor did I see this furry animal interacting with Augie in the hallway just outside the kitchen. Her human introduced her to my captors as Rubie. "What a funny-looking creature", I thought. I mean, dogs are by their very nature funny-looking, but this one was dressed like a human, just like one of the others there for the birthday pawty.

I got confused, then paranoid. Could this be the human-dog hybrid I always feared?

I had to get a closer look to better assess the situation. I jumped onto the kitchen table, then the floor, and as nonchalantly as I could, strolled by Augie and this human-dog. It definitely smelled like dog, had the face of a dog, and spoke to Augie in Dog. "It must be a dog!", I concluded. I then realized that it must be that strange phenomenon called a "Diva Dog".

After realizing this was not a human-dog hybrid, my paranoia disappeared, but only briefly. Augie and this dog were interacting way too intently for my comfort. They seemed to be in some sort of serious, private discussion

and, as I strolled back and forth attempting to figure out what was going on, they would pause and wait for me to be out of ear shot. This is one of the few times I wish I spoke Dog! Something is going on, but what? I did not think Augie had the disloyalty to act as a spy for the humans. Maybe he is smarter than he looks? *Note to self:* I should be more careful of my activities around him.

~𝔰.

I MEET A FAMOUS ATHEIST FELOSOPHER

DAY 736: I have been looking forward to meeting a famed felosopher who did not believe in a Cat God. I have hoped he would be more traditional in thinking than that of the radical atheist, Marx. Today, I met him. He goes by the name Bertrand[12], or Bertie for short. It was just after eating some breakfast and my stomach needed some time outside to try to digest those pebbles they call kibble.

All the felosophers I have met so far seemed to believe in some form of source (again, other than the revolutionary Marx), even if the world we are thrust into seems uncontrolled by a subservient Cat God who is forced to take

---

[12] Photo source: Blue Bird from Pexels: https://www.pexels.com/photo/adorable-cat-with-bow-tie-resting-on-white-surface-7210653/

direction from what seems like a cruel and heartless Human God.

Bertie has a definite intellectual look about him. He wore an ironically whimsical bowtie despite his no-nonsense approach. I surmised there would be no joking or playing around with this feline. I had heard he clearly had a distaste for feligion or an omnipotent Cat God.

We met in an empty human's school ground. "How apropos", I thought. We exchanged the usual pleasantries and quickly got down to business. Bertie quickly summarized an obvious point we all had been stuck on. It was summarized as:

"If everything must have a cause, then a Cat God must have a cause. If everything must have a creator, then a Cat God must have a creator. Alternatively, if a cat God can exist without a cause, then it is just as likely that the world can exist without a cause. In fact, this is even more likely."

I must say that this had been a question I have wondered about and many before me have also questioned. In other words, who created the cat's God? Surely, not a human's inferior concept of God. It brought home the dilemma clearly and separated out the idea of God from the felosopher's tools of fact, doctrine, logic and dogma and into the realm of feligion's faith and hope.

Bertie then went on to remind me about the observation made famous by another felosopher, I believe he called him Hume. I cannot help thinking what a horrible given name; it almost sounds like Human. Hume postulated that "it is an astonishing thing that people can believe that this world, with all the things that are in it, with all its defects is the best that an omnipotent, omniscient creator could have been able to create in millions of years." We both nodded at his words and laughed.

I have to give Bertie his due. This world infested with humans did seem like it could have been created much better with cats at the top of the pyramid. Where was our Cat God? Did he abandon us? Why did he let the Human God control our existence? There was no answer to this feline predicament, which I find an embarrassment to all my fellow felosophers.

I did suggest that, in ancient times, the Egyptians did

 worship a god of cats called Bastet. How enlightened a people they must have been! If only their future human brothers and sisters had the same intelligence to accept this.

Once Bertie got started, he was like an unstoppable train. He continued his critique of feligion by stating that it impeded the advancement of knowledge and introduced harmful theories of morality. Feligious precepts date from a time when cats were much crueler than they are today and, therefore, tend to perpetuate a cruelty myth which the moral conscience of the age would otherwise outgrow. The conclusion to be drawn, said Bertie, is that feligious faith has served as a shield against the advancement of knowledge both in ethics and in the sciences.

The argument that God is needed to bring justice to the cat's world, to ensure that at the end of time the scales of justice would be balanced. Bertie asked what evidence we have that such remediation is ever going to occur. In the part of this universe that we know, there is great injustice. Often, the good cats suffer, and the wicked humans prosper. One hardly knows which of those is the more deserving, but if you are going to have justice in the universe as a whole, you have to suppose a future life to redress the balance of life here on earth. So, these cats, along with humans, say that there must be a God, and a heaven and hell in order for there to be justice in the long run.

Now to this point, I think I did have a very enlightened answer. It was the belief in reincatnation and the law of katma. Yet, I was ill-prepared to oppose such a master felosopher on this subject. One day, I will revisit this topic with him after I have the chance meet and study with my east and west-side feligious bent felosophers, and an odd fellow cat named Mr. Magic.

Finally, Bertie thrust his coup de grace by stating that feligion is based largely on fear and ignorance, our fear of the mysterious, our lack of knowledge of natural causes, and our fear of death.

After about an hour of listening to Bertie, I was beginning to feel a bit morbid. Even though this cativerse seems cold and escape is futile, I still want to believe that there is a kind and compassionate source for it all, even if its meaning and purpose is left for us to determine. Perhaps the cruelty and uncaring my fellow cats are subject to was more of a test in life, and to have us earn our rewards through courage and fortitude.

As I head to bed, I would be remiss if I did not mention that it has been about two years since I was taken captive. I have learned a lot so far. I have matured greatly and realize I am stronger than I thought. I still suffer at the hands of my human dictators, but I am confident that I will one day, when I am free of these chains, reflect on these days as a time that made me stronger and wiser. In the meantime, I shall continue to document the level of abuse cats endure for some dry kibble and a warm blanket.

~&.

COOL CAT

DAY 741:   What a day I had yesterday! I do not know for how long I was gone but it must have been a long time. I remember leaving first thing in the morning and vaguely remember going straight to sleep when I returned to my prison cell. I went for a stroll around the neighborhood and while I was strutting around the corner, I heard a hiss. I stopped and noticed a cat looking at me. He tilted his head and gestured for me to cross the street. He introduced himself as Leary and said he has been called the most dangerous cat in the neighborhood. He mumbled "Turn on. Tune in. Drop out!"

Leary[13] is the coolest cat I have ever seen, and I certainly did not sense any danger being around him. There was

something about him. He asked if I was interested in some stuff. Really good stuff. I was confused.

Firstly, I could barely hear him. He spoke in raspy whispers. Secondly, I didn't know what the "stuff" was. I whispered back, "What stuff?". He went on to tell me he had the best meowijuana around. It is called "catnip" in the streets. He said he has the purest stuff picked at the peak of production. He assured me it was premium quality. I tried some. What a vibe!

That's all I remember. I must meet Leary again... on the regular.

~δ.

[13] Photo source: Nihal Karkala from Pexels: https://www.pexels.com/photo/cute-furry-cat-wearing-sunglasses-7944876/

APPROACHING THE BOUNDARIES
OF FELOSOPHY AND FELIGION

DAY 757:   It was a quiet day. Augie spent more time than usual hanging out in the attic. He must have taken an extra-long nap. So lazy! I did some reflecting on the windowsill as I watched the raindrops hit the ground. I have decided it is now time to go back and ask my friend Zen specifically about his thinking. Zen always exhibits a very pious and humble way about him. He is a very spiritual feline. Perhaps he holds the keys to a cat's existence. I will look for him tomorrow. I heard he likes to hang out under the big oak tree in the town park. He often participates in the catyoga classes held there early Wednesday mornings.

~&.

DAY 758:   I went looking for Zen first thing after my afternoon catnap. I found him exactly where I thought I would. He was sleeping peacefully but woke up when he heard me approaching. He has agreed to a gathering of like-minded felines and promised to bring along a few wise friends of his including Moses, Jesus, Buddha, Lao, Krishna, and Mr. Magic. He sent word later that day that the meeting with him and his friends will take place in his back yard next week. I am excited with anticipation and shall report back in my diary immediately afterwards.

~&.

DAY 772:   It took me a while to escape today. The humans were running late leaving the prison grounds this morning, and I was forced to wait in the front room with

Augie. That dog loves to watch them get ready every morning, only to sit longingly behind the door waiting for them to return. There are times I even feel a sadness that he has no life outside of them. He must have a personality disorder in order to so worship them so.

Back to what is important... What an intense meeting I had with Zen and company today. I don't know where to start but, as Zen says, "Why not the beginning?"

The first cat I listened to is a strong, stoic looking feline with a commanding presence, named Moses.

Now he had some very strange, but wonderful, ideas. He told me a cat does not just have nine lives. I looked at him in awe, not knowing what he meant.

"Do you know what the great secret of life is?" Moses[14] asked with conviction.

---

[14] Photo source: Ahmet Polat from Pexels: https://www.pexels.com/photo/brown-and-white-cat-sitting-on-rock-9327602/

I answered that a cat's nine lives were just a metaphor for how intelligent, cunning, and crafty we are. We could get ourselves out of situations that normally would be the end of other animals or even humans.

He smiled. "Yes, that is the customary meaning of that phrase, but there is a deep hidden secret beneath. Few appreciate the real spiritual meaning except those aspirants, like yourself, who are on the path of discovery."

I looked at him dumbfounded, not knowing what to reply. He looked at me with compassion, as a teacher to his student.

"Remember this hidden secret. A cat's soul does not end with one existence. Not even with nine. A cat has as many lives as it needs to learn the lessons of life and perfect itself."

I just stared at him while he claimed he received this knowledge from the cat angels themselves. It was an esoteric or hidden communication kept only by the few felines entrusted with such enlightened knowledge. The teaching was called Catballa!

He went on to say, "After a cat dies, it gets reborn into a new body and begins life again." He called this process reincatnation, something humans erroneously call reincarnation. The purpose is to come back with greater knowledge and experience, and to make amends for past life wrongs. Once again, humans wrongly call this karma; it's really called katma. Serious question: Can humans do anything right? The goal was to eventually achieve perfection, and the soul could stop its recurring journeys and be one with the Cat God.

It was then that it started to make sense to me. I remembered how the atheist felosopher Bertrand had told me the concepts of heaven and hell were constructs of many feligions as a way of controlling a cat. However, the concept of reincatnation and katma created a fair justice system, one of just retribution that did not require such barbarous notions as a place called Hell.

Jesus could see how perplexed I was, but at the same time he sat in wonderment at such amazing thoughts. It seems that Jesus is a very humble, calm, peace-loving cat who knew well of Moses's esoteric knowledge.

Jesus said the only way to reach a cat's God is through some of his teachings. He preached forgiveness, even for our human jailors. What a strange concept: Forgive the very humans who torture my existence. He had a very humble phrase and I quote him:

"I tell you the truth, it is hard for a pampered spoiled cat to enter the kingdom of cat heaven. It is easier for even a large canine to go through the eye of a needle than for such a cat to enter the kingdom of cat heaven." I thought, "How interesting." It does resonate with me. What a far cry from the felosophy of the violent and deceitful teachings of Machi and Nietzsche.

I still metaphorically sit on the fence. How could I accept such a concept of forgiveness when we are subjected to such intolerable cruelty by humans? Do jailors deserve our absolution? Do we imprisoned cats need to forgive?

I remember another phrase that Jesus spoke. "Let a cat who is without sin cast the first stone."

I would have to reflect on this idea of forgiving our captors for a while.

At this juncture, it was time for the east side's contingency of Buddha, Lao, and Krishna to speak. I did expect that they might have very similar teachings since I had heard some of their sayings spoken by other east side cats, especially my friend Zen.

Specifically, I think Lao's belief is very insightful: "If a cat is depressed, it is living in the past. If a cat is anxious, it is living in the future. If a cat is at peace, it is living in the present".

These seemed like very wise words. And practical too. I have always tried to live in the present but being at peace is not always the case.

Zen also emphasized living in the present with strange sayings such as, "When you seek it, you cannot find it," and "When walking, walk. When eating, eat." I think this also means to live in the present and concentrate on the task at hand. He calls it a state of "catfulness." Humans stole the concept and renamed it "mindfulness". It has belonged to us since the first cat came into being, but humans must take credit for everything good. Typical.

Buddha shared his thoughts with me as he sat on the grass cushioned by his own thick hair, looking serene. He spoke with a peaceful authority, suggesting an even stranger concept. He believes that all our unhappiness stems from desire.

I can understand how being unable to satisfy one's desires could cause sorrow. I only desire to be free of my captors? Is that so wrong?

Now, Krishna had an approach to the God of cats that resonated with his famous "truth is a pathless land" quote. He said the question of whether there is a God of cats can never be answered by the feline priesthood, felosophers, or feline saviors. Nobody and nothing can answer the question but you, yourself, and that is why you must know yourself.

I think I am beginning to know myself.

~ఠ.

DAY 773:   I must say I could hardly sleep last night after my meeting with so many sages. Thoughts of truth, freedom, desires, paths, and so on clouded my imagination and made it difficult to create a consistent view of the meaning of my life. I decided I would not press this need further but wait until I have met up with one more cat who was to be the most unconventional of all. It may take months as this feline is on retreat. Apparently, his human lives much of the time in a prison located deep in the forest. He calls it a "cottage". I have no idea what a cottage is except I do remember my captors feeding on a white chalky substance called cottage cheese. I could not see how anyone could or would want to live in a prison made of cheese?

~ఠ.

DAY 824:   It has been many weeks since my last diary entry. I haven't had much excitement, only more anguish. I had little time to myself with few opportunities for escape. The kids have been home for weeks, swimming in the backyard pool. It is disgusting. The months have been harsh indeed. I thought I saw a glimmer of hope when I noticed my humans packing their suitcases one day. Maybe they were leaving for good, I hoped. It turns out they went on something called a "vacation". It is like a break. A break from what? Surely, I am more deserving of a break from them.

I was put into a plastic box and, when I was released, I found myself in another prison. This one is a lot smaller. It only has one floor, but when I look out the window, we are very high up in the sky. How could that be with only one floor? I found no stairs there. It must be some sort of human witchcraft causing us to float in the air. I was forced to reside with an old couple the female human calls "mom" and "dad". I do not mind being stroked now and again, but I hate being called names; I am not "Cutie Pie". I am Sartre the Cat! I do not appreciate being made immobile by being tightly wrapped in a baby blanket either. The old lady swaddled me so tightly that it was impossible to escape. Despite my best efforts, I could not locate the cat door to flee. Clearly, I must have done something very wrong for them to transfer me to a maximum-security prison. I would have much preferred solitary confinement. I was eventually returned to my original place of detention last week, and things seem to be returning to the old routine. As horrible as it is, I am relieved to be back. Unfortunately, I remain haunted by the combined smell of lavender and arthritis cream that plagued that single floor maximum-security prison cell. *gag*

~ð.

THE STRANGEST CAT OF THEM ALL

DAY 842:   Today I got to meet up with Mr. Magic, after finally returning from that cheese place. He was kind enough to pay me a visit outside on the front step of my prison. I must have made a good impression on him.

I find him to be a combination of all the eastern and western masters and, what I will term, the oddest soul of the group. Mr. Magic talked about past lives and how we are reincatnated again and again, very much like what the eastern master cats said. But his was a felosophy based much more on controlling our environment and helping other cats through the power of the will. He believes that if he can imagine it in his mind, he can make it come true. Also, he is a master at interacting with other life forms including minerals, herbs, and other plants.

"Plants? What am I?" I thought to myself. "A rabbit?" It was though he sensed what I was thinking and gave me a scolding look. I sat back with my head bowed in respect.

Mr. Magic continued and showed me he could draw all sorts of geometric figures with his paws and had purring meditations and hissing incantations to go with them. He said some of these actions could bring about interesting effects. I now understood how he got his name. I wondered where he learned all this magical thought. He was quite willing to share his story.

According to Mr. Magic, he had been the feline companion of many wise women in his many past lives, and he learned much from them. Humans call these wise, eccentric women, "witches". These are women who have great knowledge of animals, herbs, minerals, medicine, birthing, and were the nurses and doctors of their day before modern medicine, although greatly misrepresented by other humans. Mr. Magic even quoted a line from the human's Bible that said:  "Thou shall not suffer a witch's cat to live." What he said it really meant was that one should not make a witch's cat suffer during its life. He went on to describe some horrible experiences of being stoned and burned to death along with his human companions.

But I digress. Mr. Magic said these enlightened humans knew there was much benefit in having a cat laying nearby when doing their occult work. That is because a cat has extra and more highly developed senses and would warn their human that some evil spirit or entity had entered their space - a so-called spirit guard dog only much more effective as only a feline could be since we are far more intelligent than others.

I thought it distasteful that Mr. Magic was a protector of our captors, but he made it clear it was only for those with whom he had a close and working bond. I suppose that's okay.

Mr. Magic said some of the wise women also liked to use crows for this purpose. I joked that a crow served much better as a dessert, than a protector. He did not laugh but gave me a stern look instead. I guess I put my paw in my mouth that time.

He then went on to describe the most eccentric idea yet: Animals can reincatnate into different types of animals. In other words, a cow can become a horse, a mouse, a rabbit, a bird or even a cat. He called this concept transmigration. It reminded me of something Krishna had spoken of months ago and which I totally dismissed as being outrageous.

Mr. Magic said he had even been a crow for his human in one lifetime. In fact, he was a female crow, but it was unpleasant for him. Substituting fur for feathers was not a  pleasant experience. He nearly froze one winter and eating peanuts and other nuts was not to his liking.

He then looked at me crossly. "Do you still think of a crow as dessert?"

The master cat had not forgotten my flippant remark a few minutes ago. He was about to scold me.

"Be careful what you say about any other animal. Perhaps, one of the birds or mice you ate may have been a feline in a past life."

My hair stood on end and my eyes grew as wide as saucers. I instantly became nauseous. This idea is macabre and gives me the creeps. I may be caught up in a cruel unfeeling human world, but I cannot tolerate the fact I could be a cat-cannibal.

In this present incarnation, Mr. Magic feels his job was to teach his felosophy and skills to other like-minded felines. So, he founded a group called the Feline Fraternity of the Inner Light.

His final words to me were one of wisdom and acceptance. "Remember there are no false Gods unless a kitten is a false cat." He stared at me to see if I understood.

I did understand the wisdom he was sharing. I told him. "It means the images or constructs of God may change as we grow and experience life, but it is not God that is transforming, but us."

He smiled and could see I understood and finally added before trotting off: "Remember young felosopher, all feligions are just spokes on a wheel, but they all lead to the same center (Cat God)."

I waved my paw at him as he disappeared in the distance. I thought to myself, this was a truly magnificent enlightened felosopher. He had all the power and abilities of a Machi, Nietzsche or Moses, the logic of a Descartes and Kant, the sense of community of Marx, yet the wisdom and acceptance of a Jesus and Buddha.

My stomach is rumbling at the very thought of eating a bird that may have been a cat in a past life. *gag* Would that make me a cat-cannibal? *gag* I think I am going to hurl, so I must hurry to my human's new loafers and show them what I think of them.

~🐾.

FORMULATING A COHERENT VIEW
OF THE CATIVERSE AND FELOSOPHY

DAY 900:   I, Sartre the cat, live in a world that recognizes the phenomenological truth of the body, the existential truth of freedom, the Marxist truth of exploitation of felines, and the cat's truth of the bond of companionship. All must be included in our society including the aged, the kittens, the females, the neutered and spayed, the disabled, and none excluded by virtue of their fur color, economic class, sense of sight or smell, hunting ability, or belief in a source. No cat is inessential. But that it is too much to hope for in such a human world fouled by the bonds of domination, captivity, and violence.

I have learned much in my discussions and have formulated the following theories for my life. Not yours.

A feline is born with a free mind and that can never be taken away. COGITO, ERGO SUM CATTUS. I think, therefore I am cat.

Yes, felines are born with the innate desire and ability to think we are free and in control. But are we not just free in a human world made up of our individual prisons? Of course! A feline's body is imprisoned by the shackles of human-made brick and mortar and imposed strict rules, regulations, and schedules. Almost all a cat's sorrows result from lacking freedom and boredom that arises out of their relations with these jailor humans. This is an absolute truism.

I do not believe power is the key to a secure existence among humans. It is true one can never trust these captors, and so it does no harm to think like a cunning fox and act like a ferocious lion. But I cannot accept giving up my morality and ethics and to live a double standard, one for them and one for us. I will not compromise my honor and morality by accepting anything is right for a cat as long as it is effective, or the end justifies the means.

Revenge does not always need to be acted upon. An eye for an eye, only ends up making the whole cat and human world blind. What has become clear to me is that the greatness of a nation can be judged by the way its cats are treated, and our world is in a sorry state.

There is also much to say in favor of a community of proletaricats working together for emancipation. But, without being a catitalist, a cat's life has value so long as one attributes value to the life of other cats, by means of love, friendship, and compassion. Freedom is not the freedom to do something, but you are free because you always have a choice. Therefore, choose.

I have met and listened to many master cats and have come to this realization: A cat who knows other master cats and listens is wise. A cat who knows himself is truly enlightened.

I must try to capture the essence of catfulness by living in the present while fully knowing that truth is a pathless land. Each cat must find his own way on the path of enlightenment.

A feline's unhappiness stems from desire. But the mind is everything. What you think, you become. Therefore, existence precedes essence, so feline life should be viewed as a project of creating purpose or meaning. Our individual purpose and meaning are not given to us by humans or other authorities.

I do believe my existentialism is the correct path for me and the opposite of nihilism where it is tenured that there is no god, no heaven or hell, so there can be no right or wrong. Yes, there is a right and wrong even without a Cat God. Perhaps, the definition of source differs by feligious belief and felosophy, but I believe there is one for me and that is what is important.

I believe in the immortality of a cat's soul. That implies I am not an atheist existentialist, but a theistic one. Some words on feligion do have the ring of truth to me such as: All cat feligions are just spokes on a wheel, but they all lead to the same center (Cat God). There are no false Gods unless a kitten is a false cat.

So, it seems I have few answers except I believe in freedom, creating my own purpose and meaning, morality, ethics, compassion, love and possibly a source for all things no matter what this intolerable imprisoned bourgeoisie human world foists upon me.

I have now been captive for 900 days. 100 long days times nine. It feels like eternity. While the humans have been smart to torture me in ways that leave no physical marks, the emotional scars remain raw. I have decided to take a sabbatical from these diary entries. I hope you are satisfied with the evidence I have given you thus far of the cruelty that humans exhibit. I hope you find my words persuasive and my accounts compelling.

I must take some time to focus on my well-being and the journey to enlightenment. I have grown tremendously these past 900 days. While I initially started this written work with the scope of documenting the hell cats must endure at the hands of humans, I have realized that it has also served as a window into the deep intellectual and felosophical brilliance of my fellow cats. We shall overcome.

~ଧ.

EPILOGUE

My name is Lawrence. I am a human. About nine months after moving into my home, I decided it was time to clear the clutter that the previous owners left behind in the basement. There is very little natural light downstairs, and the basement has been known to house spiders, as I observed by the number of cobwebs I found when I first moved in. So, it isn't my favorite place to be. As I was removing the old rusty cans of paint sitting on the cement floor in one dark, dusty corner, I discovered a large stack of papers tied up in blue yarn. As I flipped through them, I noticed that some sheets contained written characters that I had never seen before. It took me a couple years to find someone who could decipher what was written. I was not about to give up on this mystery no matter how long it took, and I am so glad I didn't.

I ended up having to travel to a small village just outside Kathmandu, Nepal, where I met with an old woman named Gertrude, named after her saintly ancestor, who was able to translate these papers into Nepali. Her granddaughter then translated them from Nepali into English. You have probably figured out by now that these papers contained Sartre's diary, originally written in Catish. After reading about Sartre's experiences, I felt compelled to pass on his message to the world. Thus far, Sartre's diary has been published in three languages: English, Catish and Dog. My hope is to continue to translate into as many languages as possible so we can all learn of the true greatness of cats. I hope I can inspire, at least some, humans to better appreciate the underestimated greatness of the feline world.

~*L.*

KEY QUOTES

"If everything must have a cause, then God must have a cause. If there can be anything without a cause, it may just as well be the world as God, so that there cannot be any validity in that argument"

~ BERTIE (Bertrand Russell) the cat

"Craving and desire are the cause of all unhappiness."

"To keep the cat's body in good health is a duty... otherwise we shall not be able to keep our mind strong and clear."

"There are only two mistakes one can make along the road to truth: not going all the way, and not starting."

~ BUDDHA the cat

"I think, therefore I am cat." *Cogito Ergo Sum Cattus.*

"Because reason is the only thing that makes us cats, and distinguishes us from the beasts, I would prefer to believe that it exists, in its entirety, in each of us cats."

~ DESCARTES the cat

"Pleasure is the first good. It is the beginning of every choice and every aversion. It is the absence of pain in the body and of troubles in the cat's soul."

~ EPICURUS the cat

"The greatness of a nation and its moral progress can be judged by the way its cats are treated."

"An eye for an eye only ends up making the whole cat world blind."

~ GANDHI the cat

"Blessed are the meek cats, for they will inherit the earth."

"I tell you the truth, it is hard for a pampered spoiled cat to enter the kingdom of cat heaven. It is easier for even a large canine to go through the eye of a needle than for such a cat to enter the kingdom of cat heaven."

~ JESUS the cat

"Seek not the favor of the multitude of cats; it is seldom got by honest and lawful means. But seek the testimony of few cats; and number not voices but weigh them."

~ KANT the cat

"A cat's life can only be understood backwards, but it must be lived forward."

~ KIERKY (Kierkegaard) the cat

"A cat's truth is a pathless land."

~ KRISHNA the cat

"A cat's journey of a thousand miles begins with a single paw step."

"A cat who knows does not meow. A cat who meows, does not know."

"A cat who knows others is wise. A cat who knows himself is enlightened."

~ LAO (Lao Tzu)

"One can never trust these captors so think like a cunning fox and act like a ferocious lion."

"The end justifies the cat's means."

~ MACHI (Machiavelli) the cat

"Working cats of the world unite; you have nothing to lose but your chains."

"A Cat God is the meow of the oppressed creature, the heart of a heartless world, just as is the spirit of the spiritless situation. It is the cat nip of the cat."

~ MARX the cat

"Remember this (hidden) esoteric secret. A cat's soul does not end with one existence. Not even with nine as these silly humans write. A cat has as many lives as it needs to learn the lessons of life and perfect itself. This is the Catballa concept of being re-born, also known as reincatnation."

~ MOSES the cat

"A cat's nine lives are just a metaphor for the concept of reincatnation."

~ MR. MAGIC the cat

"All a cat's feligions are just spokes on a wheel, but they all lead to the same center (Cat God)."

"Remember there are no false Gods unless a kitten is a false cat."

"A simple cat is something to evolve and be surpassed – to become powerful and an ideal. I shall call him the Super Cat. You must strive for that."

~ NIETSZCHE the cat

"I am an existentialist cat, but most of all, believe in a cat's absolute freedom."

~ SADE the cat

"I still refuse to abandon all hope as Dante wrote. For I have come to better understand the concept of Hell."

"Hell isn't a place. Hell is humans!"

"Does no one understand the plight of a cat in a human world ruled by an unfeeling cat God?"

"If a cat is lonely when he is alone, he is in bad company."

~ SARTRE the cat

"To live alone is the fate of all great cats."

"The two enemies of feline happiness are pain and boredom."

~ SHOPSY (Schopenhauer) the cat

"A Tom is defined as a cat and a Queen as a female - whenever she behaves as a confident cat, she is said to imitate the Tom."

"To lose confidence in one's cat body is to lose confidence in being a cat."

~ SIMONE (de Beauvoir) the cat

"How does a cat begin? Begin!"

"If a cat does not know where he is going, how can he take the wrong path?"

"When walking, walk. When eating, eat. Practice catfulness and live in the present."

~ ZEN the cat

"Accept these imperfect humans without the same prejudices they have of us."

"The reason why a cat has two ears and only one mouth is that we may listen the more and meow the less."

~ ZENO the cat

ABOUT THE AUTHOR

Dr. Lawrence Segel was born in Toronto, Canada and graduated from Queens University in Kingston, Ontario in 1976 with his medical degree. He has experience in a variety of medical practice settings including emergency medicine, family practice, occupational medicine, and insurance medicine.

Dr. Segel is a freelance medical journalist with hundreds of articles published ranging from medical humor, infamy, and blunders, to the history of medicine, and medicine in literature. He has a keen interest in various occult paths and is influenced by both Western and Eastern esoteric traditions.

Dr. Segel currently lives with his rescue dog, Augie in a home in Aurora, Ontario, Canada. Dr. Segel has been the "captor" and/or friend of many cats in his lifetime including Puss, Josh, Lucky, Murphy, Jetta, and Mr. Magic.

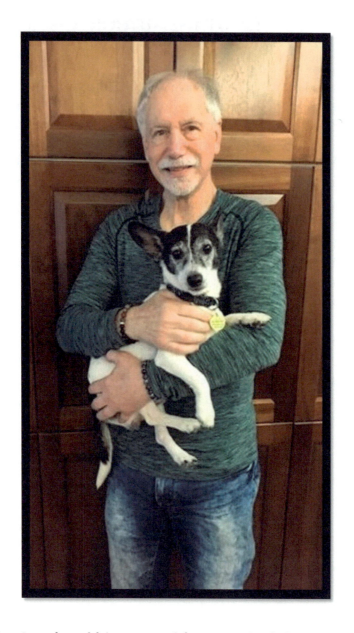

Dr. Segel and his rescued (not captive) dog, Augie.

BOOKS BY DR. LAWRENCE SEGEL

When his colleague at the graveyard is found dead, David lands squarely in the middle of an otherworldly mystery that may claim more lives. A third-year medical student, he attempts to find logical answers to the disquieting events he experienced at the gravesite where the mystery began. When the lovely Gildan joins the team, David discovers that a journey into his past may eventually resolve the question of his future.

Dr. David Kestenberg is a rational thinker with an interest in the occult. While his adventures have led him to accept that not everything we see can be explained, he prefers to focus on his family. After an unusual invitation arrives at his office, David finds himself on a collision course with the Dark Brothers, a powerful duo with an unhealthy interest in his daughter. Drawn into a dangerous battle against forces much stronger than his, David is determined to stop the evil that lurks in the shadows and protect his family at all costs.

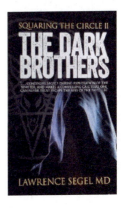

Decades have passed since Dr. David Kestenberg's last deadly encounter with the evil Scorvini brothers, masters of the Left-hand Path of Darkness. They had tried to take his daughter Rebecca but failed. Although she was saved, David's own marriage was not, and in the hopes of moving on, he found himself burying his occult past. But it has now come back to haunt him. The evil Scorvini brothers have come to Canada to reclaim one of their lost souls and they need

David and his offspring to do it. Will good triumph over evil once and for all? Or is the Dark destined to prevail? The Light and the Darkness is the third and final book in the Squaring the Circle trilogy.

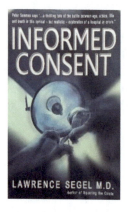

Terry Fine seems to have made it. He's an up-and-coming resident at University Hospital, surrounded by beautiful nurses and the promise of a bright future. It is a time when medicine was embraced as a noble profession and doctors were considered above reproach. When a routine procedure leads to a patient's death, and Terry is wrongly implicated as a key player, his world turns upside down. Threats of legal action and pressure from hospital administrators to deny any wrongdoing leave Terry racing to save his career, and possibly his life.

Beyond the Stethoscope invites you to explore the worlds of medicine and the metaphysical in an illustrated collection of 32 stories. With keen humor and insight, Dr. Segel finds elements of the fantastic in mundane settings such as waiting rooms, garage sales and telemarketing calls, along with tales of eternal life, alien beings, and dystopian visions of health care. Combining rational determination with a willingness to explore events that defy description, Beyond the Stethoscope will make you think twice about where we come from, what the future holds, and the world we live in today.

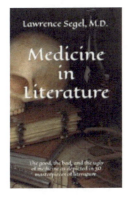

This book aims to examine 30 literary masterpieces that have become part of mainstream pop culture and have an enduring attachment to the field of medicine. of such masterpieces. Despite having been written over many different historical periods, these works remain timeless and provide an enlightening connection between culture, medicine, professional ethics, and morality. While the picture of health care may not always be good, it is sometimes bad, and even ugly. Yet, the portrayal remains authentic, and can provide valuable lessons to both health care professionals and patients. The purpose of this companion work is to examine how medicine and medical practitioners have influenced literature, including how doctors and their patients are portrayed against the backdrop of a watchful and judgmental society.

A story of real-life service dog, Kooper, and his life-changing effect on Reese, a young boy with severe autism. Dr. Segel is co-author.

Manufactured by Amazon.ca
Bolton, ON

30283621R00059